My Forever Friendship Pony

Story by
Jane Hansen

Illustrated by
Mitchell Newson

Inspired by Adriana Hansen

Seeds of Insight
PUBLISHING

Published by

Seeds of Insight

PUBLISHING

Parkland, Florida

ISBN: 978-0-6159546-5-3

Editor: Carol Rosenberg · www.carolkillmanrosenberg.com
Cover and interior design: Gary A. Rosenberg · www.thebookcouple.com

Printed in the United States

This book is dedicated to
my beautiful daughter Adriana,
whose happy, outgoing spirit
makes every day brighter.

It was a breezy, sunny day when Anabelle decided to crawl under a large Gumbo Limbo tree and hug her stuffed pony, Little Rock. Normally, Anabelle would be zooming around playing tag with her friends, swinging on her hammock, or catching monarch butterflies in the garden.

But today, for some reason, she was feeling a bit lonely and sad—
and maybe even a little angry.

Anabelle wasn't sure why she was
feeling like this. Was she tired?
Was there something she wanted?
Was she hungry? Was it because
there was someone that she missed?
Yes, that's it, she thought to herself.
She was missing someone who
couldn't be with her right now.

With that thought in her mind, Anabelle snuggled with Little Rock. He was, after all, her favorite stuffed animal. She carried him with her whenever she needed to feel safe and loved. His caramel-colored fur felt soft against her arms and even though Little Rock was only a stuffed animal, she felt protected when he was nearby.

As Little Rock lay in Anabelle's arms and the wind swept across her face, she closed her eyes and began to drift into a daydream. She imagined herself surrounded by friends and family, by people who loved her. She was imagining not feeling lonely and sad anymore. She even imagined not feeling angry about this either.

While deep in thought and enjoying her daydream, Anabelle suddenly heard the sound of a pony neighing. She quickly sprung her eyes open and couldn't believe what she saw before her.

There stood the most beautiful multicolored pony glistening in the sunlight. From his tail all the way to his nose, he was all the colors of the rainbow. His tail was cherry red, and his body was pumpkin orange, sunshine yellow, and bright plum purple. His legs were the color of blueberries and green grass. Even his mane looked like a rainbow you would see in the sky after a rainy day.

Although he was no longer caramel colored, Anabelle had no doubt that this pony was really Little Rock who had come to life!

Anabelle stared in disbelief as her beautiful blue eyes gazed at this miracle. She stuttered in amazement to Little Rock, "Wh . . . wh . . . what happened? How did you become real?"

A smile spread across Little Rock's face, as he answered, "I see you're having some mixed up feelings, Anabelle, and I am here to help you. It's okay to feel angry and sad. These feelings are part of life, and if we never know anger and sadness, then we would never know true happiness! But we don't want those feelings to stay around too long. So I have to come to share three special messages with you that I want you to always remember."

Speechless, Anabelle smiled and nodded her head. Silently, she told her pony that she was ready to hear the messages.

Nodding back at her, Little Rock began, "The first thing I want you to know is that even if you are separated from people who you love, you are always connected by special heartstrings."

"These invisible heartstrings connect you with your loved ones. Your heart can feel their heart and their heart can feel yours. This is important to remember to help you through your feelings."

"Remember, Anabelle, it's okay to feel these things. When you are missing someone you love, your feelings tell you it is not okay that the person you love is not with you. This can cause you to feel angry and sad. Remember, the heartstrings will always help keep you connected to the ones you love, even if they are not with you."

Anabelle thought about what Little Rock said. She closed her eyes for a moment and imagined the people she was missing. All of a sudden, a warm, peaceful feeling came over her. *She felt it! She felt the heartstrings! Little Rock was right!*

"What's the next message? Please tell me," Anabelle pleaded as she gazed at her colorful friend.

Little Rock continued, "You are a beautiful light that shines brightly. Whenever you need to feel happy or safe, look inside yourself and you will find all that you need. Breathe deeply and know that you are amazing and magnificent."

Anabelle smiled at Little Rock as she took a deep breath and thought about this second message. She thought about the trees, the flowers, the wind, and how beautiful they were, and how beautiful Little Rock was with his rainbow-colored fur.

Then she realized, if all this that she saw around her was beautiful, then she must also be a part of it. She must also be beautiful!

Anabelle knew right then and there that she could find her
own peace and happiness just by looking within herself!
Yes, Little Rock was right once again!

Finally, Little Rock asked Anabelle if she was ready to hear
the last message he had come to share with her.

"Yes, I am ready. Please tell me," Anabelle responded as she anxiously waited to hear his reply.

Little Rock held his head high, and he continued, "The last message I want to share is about ME. Even if you can't hear me talk or see me move, I am here for you. I will be your forever friend so keep me close to you whenever you need a special hug."

With a happy heart, Anabelle reached out and gave Little Rock a huge hug. Once again she closed her eyes and felt the love her pony had for her. Just then, while in her arms, Anabelle felt Little Rock turn back into the caramel-colored stuffed pony she adored.

For a moment Anabelle felt sad. She almost started to miss Little Rock, with his rainbow fur and friendly voice. But then she remembered Little Rock's three messages.

First, she felt her heartstrings connecting her to him! Then, she recalled Little Rock telling her that she didn't have to keep those sad feelings. She had the power within herself to find joy and happiness.

She smiled at that thought. Then looking down at Little Rock, she realized that even though she couldn't hear him speak to her or could not hear his voice anymore, and even though he was not moving, she could still hold him in her arms and feel his special friendship.

She knew from that moment on, Little Rock really would be her forever friend.

THE END

A Note to Parents and Guardians about Children's Grief

It is important to know or remember that children are unique in the ways they grieve. Children may not know what they are feeling or how to put those feelings into words. Children do, however, express their feelings by showing you how they feel with their behavior.

It can be frustrating and difficult to have empathy for a child when you see a child "angry" and/or acting out with bad behaviors. It is important to not shame a child for their "angry" behaviors. Instead, help them by labeling the behaviors with the feelings that match.

When a child doesn't have the awareness or the words to express these feelings of loss, the labeling of these behaviors are helpful in moving past them. Identifying the anger and asking what is not okay with the child is a way to validate his or her feelings. This helps to prevent the child from experiencing shame for their natural stage of grieving. Once you have established this understanding, you are now in the position to offer some supportive and comforting words. Anger is a helpful emotion if you think about what its purpose is. Anger says, "Hey, this is not okay with me."

Whether a child experiences his or her loss by someone moving away, dying, or abandonment, his or her stages of grief are similar. If a child's behavior does not improve over time with support, compassion, and love, please don't hesitate to consult with a mental healthcare professional who specializes in children's grief and bereavement.

—Shari B. Kaplan, LCSW
sharibkaplan@me.com

About the Inspiration

Adriana Hansen is an outgoing, happy, spirited seven-year-old. She has a great passion for horses and rides weekly. Adriana also enjoys spending time playing with her dog, Jack, and her bunny, Shortcake. When Adriana's mom had the idea to help children with their sad and angry feelings, Adriana told her that rainbow-colored ponies would be perfect. And that is how this book came to be. Ever since this idea developed, Adriana and her parents have been collecting stuffed ponies of all shapes and colors to be partnered with the book. They will donate the ponies and books to children who are in foster care, as these children have all experienced some sort of loss in their lives. It is their hope that this book and the ponies will, on some level, help the children heal their hearts.

For more information about donating ponies,
please contact myforeverfriendshippony@gmail.com

About the Author

Jane Hansen has enjoyed a twenty-year career as an elementary school teacher. She has also served as a certified parenting instructor of the Redirecting Children's Behavior course. She is the proud mother of three children, John and Jennifer (both of whom are grown adults) and Adriana, who just began first grade.

Jane enjoys cooking, yoga, and learning about holistic health. Jane lives with her husband, Mark, and their daughter, Adriana, in Parkland, Florida.

About the Illustrator

Mitchell Newson is originally from Long Island, New York. He moved to Florida in 2001 and currently resides in Delray Beach. Mitchell spends his time illustrating, as well as building, restoring, and playing guitars. He lives with his wife, Lauren, and his dog, Jack.

You can contact Mitchell at mitchellnewsonillustrations @gmail.com.